To Nicholas
KAREL HAYES
2010

Snowflake
Comes to Stay

Karel Hayes

Down East

This book is dedicated
with love to my sisters,
Kathryn and Karen Anne Hayes
(or as I know them, Kath and Mimi),
and always with love for Brent.

Also with grateful thanks to my friend
Ellen Barolak, for her suggestions
and help with the French phrases.

And of course many thanks to
my dog, Snowy!

Copyright © 2010 by Karel Hayes

ISBN 978-0-89272-850-3

Designed by Lynda Chilton

Printed in China, June 2010
5   4   3   2   1

BOOKS·MAGAZINE·ONLINE
w w w . d o w n e a s t . c o m
Distributed to the trade by National Book Network

Library of Congress Cataloging-in-Publication Data

Hayes, Karel, 1949-
   Snowflake comes to stay / by Karel Hayes. -- 1st ed.
      p. cm.
   Summary: Harriet Harrington is an author who lives alone in a little house
in the north woods and prefers it that way, until her friend Monique
convinces her to bring a Bichon Frise puppy home for just one week.
   ISBN 978-0-89272-850-3 (hardcover : alk. paper)
   [1. Authors--Fiction. 2. Bichon frise--Fiction. 3. Dogs--Fiction. 4.
Animals--Infancy--Fiction.] I. Title.
   PZ7.H31476Sno 2010
      [E]--dc22
                        2010005296

Harriet Harrington lived alone in a little house in the woods, on the shore of a lake, in the shadow of a mountain. The house, the woods, the lake, and the mountain were all in a village far to the north in a northern state.

Harriet didn't mind being alone, because she was an author and was always busy writing. She wrote and wrote. She wrote all the time, until one day, when nothing she wrote was right.

Harriet was worried. She needed to write the ending to her newest book.

Days passed, then a week, and still Harriet hadn't written the ending.

On Friday she received a phone call from her friend Monique, who raised little white dogs.

"Mon amie," said Monique. "I have the dog for you, *très jolie!"*

Monique had been trying for years to get Harriet to take one of her dogs.

"No thank you," said Harriet. "I don't need a dog, I'm too busy writing."

"It is a new year, Harriet, you need to make some changes," said Monique. "You need to get a dog. Harriet, this is the dog for you. The other dogs, I was mistaken, but this is the dog for you."

This time Monique would not take no for an answer, and before Harriet knew it, she agreed to take the dog.

"But only for one week," she added quickly.

"Oh, but of course, *ma chère,*" said Monique, who knew that once a person held a puppy and brought that puppy home with them, that puppy did not come back. "Come to my house tomorrow," she added. *"A bientôt"*

That night it snowed and snowed . . .

. . . so in the morning Harriet had
to snowshoe to Monique's house to
get the dog.

"She's so little,"
exclaimed Harriet. "She's no
bigger than a snowflake."

"Snowflake! *Magnifique!*"
said Monique. "That is
the perfect name for this
little one."

"You take the dog for
a week," said Monique,
smiling. "And I will come to
your house next Saturday, a
week from today."

Harriet returned
home with Snowflake and
all of Snowflake's things.

Harriet put Snowflake in the kitchen and Snowflake, who was just a puppy, immediately had an accident.

Harriet put her outside.

Snowflake explored her new home. She found
all of her things where Harriet had put them.

There were many things that Snowflake liked and many things she didn't like. She didn't like dog food, but she loved spaghetti noodles.

She didn't like vacuum cleaners,

but she loved scarves, slippers, mittens, paper, and even the dictionary.

She loved Harriet's big chair, especially when Harriet was in the chair. And she loved Harriet's big bed, but she was not allowed in the bed.

Snowflake really, really loved Harriet's big bed.

Now even though Harriet did not allow Snowflake in
her bed, they did do everything else together and the days
of the week passed quickly.

Harriet even began writing again, working very hard to finish the ending to her book, and Snowflake worked very hard to help her.

Snowflake was so excited to finally
be in Harriet's bed, she . . .

"Thank goodness for washing machines," said Harriet.

At the end of the week Harriet finished her book. She was very happy. She thought it was the best book with the best ending she had ever written.

Snowflake was happy too. That night they had a party. They ate
spaghetti noodles and played hide and seek. Snowflake was much
better at the game than Harriet.

At bedtime Harriet fell asleep
right away, but Snowflake was too
excited to fall asleep.

The Story
by
Harriet Harrington

The next morning . . .

. . . Snowflake went back
to stay with Monique.

After Snowflake left, Harriet sat alone at her desk and tried to put her book back together.

She sat alone at her table and tried to eat.

She sat alone in her chair and tried to read.

It was a long day and an even longer night.

Harriet couldn't fall asleep. Then, in the middle of the night, she realized what was wrong. She, Harriet Harrington, who had never been lonely before, was lonely.

She missed the little white dog. She missed Snowflake. She decided to go to Monique's house the next morning.

But the next morning, there was Monique, at her front door.

"You must take her back," said Monique. "She doesn't eat, she doesn't sleep, she cries all the time. She misses you!"

"I miss her too!" cried Harriet.

"Fantastique!" exclaimed Monique, who knew all along that this would be the ending to this story, the story of how Snowflake came to stay.